I Can Read

ITTY BITTY KITTY

FIREHOUSE FUN

by Joan Holub
illustrated by James Burks

HARPER
An Imprint of HarperCollinsPublishers

It is a big day
at the firehouse.
Ava goes to visit.

So does her cat.

His name is Itty Bitty.

But he is not itty. Or bitty.

There are snacks for all
in the firehouse.
Ava gets a little snack.

Itty Bitty gets a little snack.
And another. And another.
Ah, just right.

Look!

Ava sees something wiggle.

What could it be?

A fire hose!
Firefighter Smitty
shows Ava how to spray water.

Water is an itty bitty bit too wet for a cat.

Now Itty Bitty sees
something wiggle!

What could it be?

It is a tail!
A tail that belongs
to a firehouse dog.

"MEOW," says Itty Bitty.

"GRR," says the firehouse dog.

The firehouse dog runs away.

Does he want to play chase?

Itty Bitty likes this game.
The firehouse dog
does not like it.
Not one itty bitty bit!

Off they go!
Itty Bitty runs past
hats, coats, and boots.

Where is that firehouse dog?

Is he up here?

Is he down there?

Itty Bitty goes down.

Itty Bitty gets stuck!

Oh, Itty Bitty.

"You are too big," says Ava.

Itty Bitty does not think
he is too big.
He thinks the hole
is too small.

Hey! There's that dog again!

It zooms away.

Itty Bitty zooms after it.

Oops!

They bump a button.

RRR-RRR

CRASH!

The firefighters hear the alarm.

They run over.

But there is not a real fire.

RRRRRRRR~

RRRRR!!!

The firehouse dog howls.

Itty Bitty howls.

"Oh, Itty Bitty," says Ava.

Now Firefighter Smitty
shows them how to stay safe
if there is a real fire.

"When smoke goes UP,
you go DOWN,"
Firefighter Smitty tells them.

Itty Bitty
and the firehouse dog
learn to be safe, too.

Itty Bitty and the dog stop,

drop,

and roll.

Now Ava and Itty Bitty
say good-bye.
Ava made a new friend today.

Itty Bitty made
a new friend, too.

Itty Bitty, what a kitty!

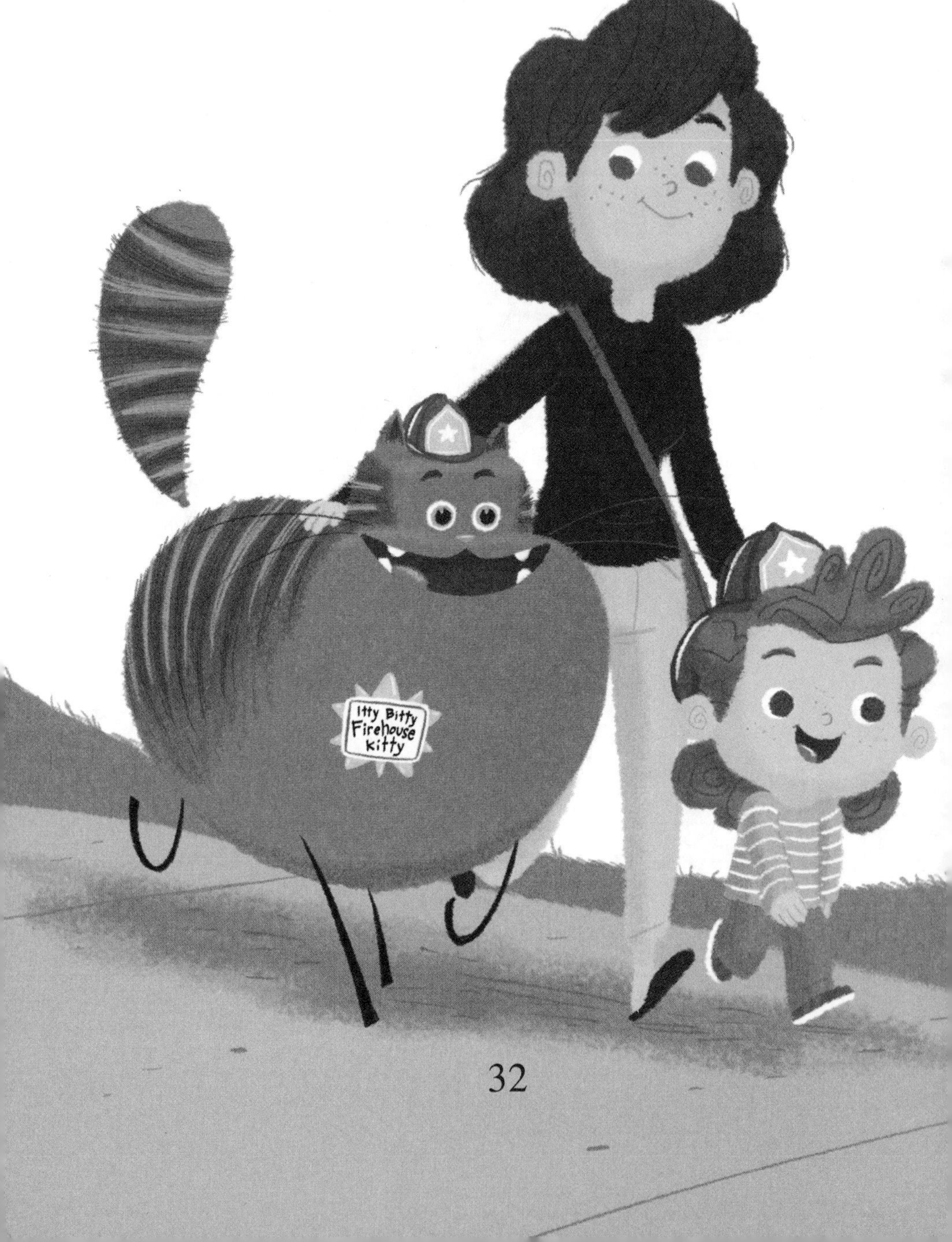